Bob the Builder™

Muck's Sleepover

adapted by **Kiki Thorpe**   based on the teleplay by **Ben Randall**   with thanks to **Hot Animation**

SIMON SPOTLIGHT
New York   London   Toronto   Sydney   Singapore

Based upon the television series *Bob the Builder*™ created by HIT Entertainment PLC
and Keith Chapman, with thanks to HOT Animation 🖐, as seen on Nick Jr.®

SIMON SPOTLIGHT
An imprint of Simon & Schuster Children's Publishing Division
1230 Avenue of the Americas
New York, New York 10020

Manufactured in the United States of America

First Edition

2 4 6 8 10 9 7 5 3 1

ISBN 0-689-84755-6

Late one afternoon Wendy, Muck, and Roley were hard at work. They were making a path through Farmer Pickles's field. While Wendy supervised, Muck cleared a trail and Roley smoothed it down.

Farmer Pickles and Travis stopped to say good-bye.
"Goodness," said Wendy. "Is it time to go home already?" Wendy and the machines had been so busy they hadn't noticed the time. "Muck, we'll have to come back and finish the job first thing in the morning."
"Oh, no!" Muck cried. "Does that mean I'll have to wake up early?"
Wendy laughed. "I'm afraid so," she said.
"I know!" Travis piped up. "Why don't you sleep at the farm tonight, Muck?"

Muck had never spent the night away from home before.

"Can I stay, Wendy? Can I pleeeease?" Muck pleaded.

"It's all right with me," said Farmer Pickles. "If it's all right with you."

"Well, okay," said Wendy. "Remember to behave yourself, Muck."

"I will, I will!" Muck promised.

"Hooray!" Travis and Muck cheered.

"Bye, everyone," Wendy said, climbing aboard Roley. "Sleep well!"

Later that evening Muck and Travis settled down in the shed.

"This is exciting!" Muck said. "I've never slept in the country before."

"Is it different from sleeping in town?" asked Travis.

"Oh, yes. In town there are cars going past," Muck told him. "And the streetlights are on all night long."

Travis yawned. "I suppose you find it dark and quiet here," he said sleepily.

Suddenly Muck noticed that it *was* very dark and quiet on Farmer Pickles's farm.

"D–D–Dark and q–q–quiet," Muck said. "Oh, dear."

Nearby, Spud was listening. "It won't be quiet for long," he said, chuckling to himself.

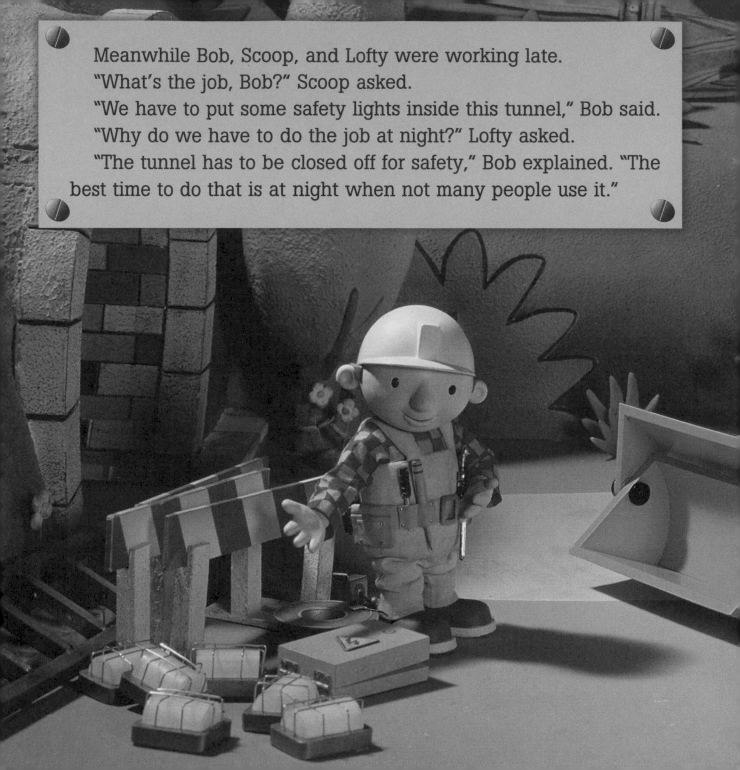

Meanwhile Bob, Scoop, and Lofty were working late.

"What's the job, Bob?" Scoop asked.

"We have to put some safety lights inside this tunnel," Bob said.

"Why do we have to do the job at night?" Lofty asked.

"The tunnel has to be closed off for safety," Bob explained. "The best time to do that is at night when not many people use it."

Inside the tunnel Bob used his drill to attach a long cable to the wall. Then he connected lights to the cable.

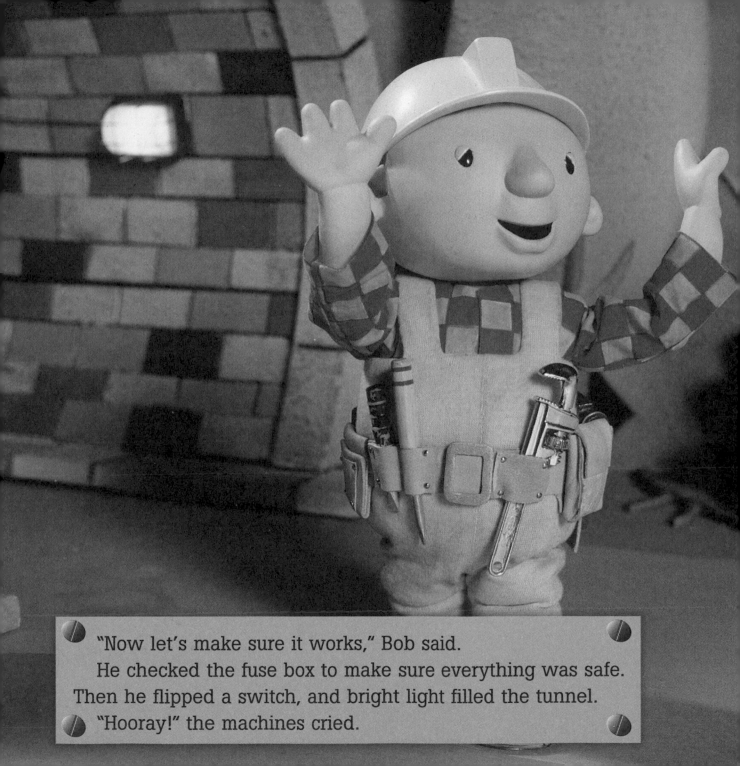

"Now let's make sure it works," Bob said.
He checked the fuse box to make sure everything was safe.
Then he flipped a switch, and bright light filled the tunnel.
"Hooray!" the machines cried.

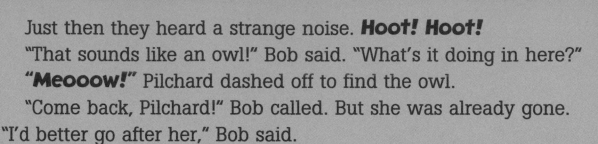

Just then they heard a strange noise. **Hoot! Hoot!**
"That sounds like an owl!" Bob said. "What's it doing in here?"
"Meooow!" Pilchard dashed off to find the owl.
"Come back, Pilchard!" Bob called. But she was already gone.
"I'd better go after her," Bob said.

Back at Farmer Pickles's farm, Muck was wide-awake.
Suddenly a twig snapped. And then another.
"What was that, Travis?" Muck asked.
"ZZZZZZZ," Travis replied, fast asleep.

"Ha, ho-ho!" Spud giggled to himself. He was having fun teasing Muck.

Spud made a spooky noise. "Whooooooooooh!"

"It's just the wind," Muck said nervously.

"Huuack! Huuuuack!" Spud called, making another scary sound.
"Ahhhh!" Muck screamed. "It's a horrible monster!" Quick as
a flash Muck zoomed out of the shed and away from the farm.
"Come back, Muck!" Spud shouted. "I haven't finished scaring you!"

Muck sped down the road and over the bridge. Suddenly, just ahead, Muck saw . . .

"BOB!" Muck hit the brakes.

"Muck! What are you doing out here?" Bob asked in surprise.

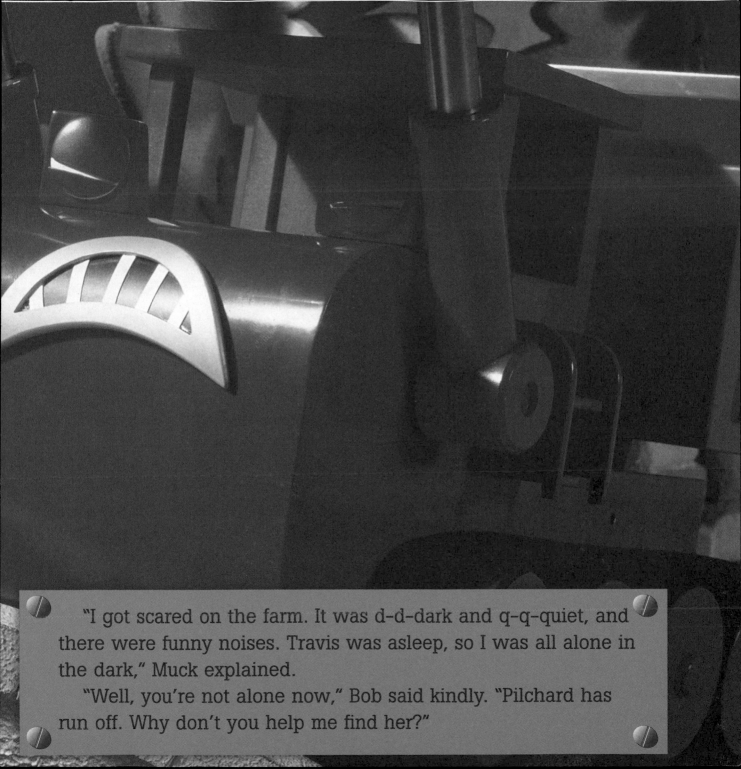

"I got scared on the farm. It was d-d-dark and q-q-quiet, and there were funny noises. Travis was asleep, so I was all alone in the dark," Muck explained.

"Well, you're not alone now," Bob said kindly. "Pilchard has run off. Why don't you help me find her?"

Nearby, Spud had lost his way in the dark. It was quiet and spooky. A bush rustled. "M-M-Muck, is that you?" Spud stammered.

"**Hoot! Hoot!**" said the owl from a nearby fence post.

"AHHHH!" Spud cried. "A hooting monster!" Spud jumped up and dashed off.

"**MEEOOW!**" screeched Pilchard, surprised.

Pilchard ran toward the road. When she spotted Bob she leaped into his arms. "Ho-ho," Bob laughed. "Where did you come from?"

"Purr, purr," said Pilchard, happy to have found her friend.

"Now we can finish the job," said Bob. "Come on, Muck, you can help."

When their work was done Bob took Muck back to Farmer Pickles's farm.

"But I won't be able to sleep in the dark," Muck said with a sigh.

"Don't worry, Muck." Bob said. "I've got a plan."

Muck settled next to the shed where Travis was sleeping.

"Good night, Muck," said Scoop and Lofty.

"Er . . . 'night, everyone," Muck said, sounding a little confused.

Then Bob pushed a button. The work lights came on, lighting up the shed as bright as day.

"Now there's no reason to be afraid of the dark!" laughed Bob.

And in no time at all Muck fell fast asleep. **"Zzzzzzz."**